THE QUEEN'S JUBILEE

Frances Rose

Once upon a time, in a land not so far away, lived a queen called Lizzie.

Queen Lizzie had been a queen for a very long time. In fact, she had been the queen for longer than any other king or queen in her kingdom. In just a couple of weeks, she was going to celebrate being on the throne for seventy years and she just couldn't wait!

Everybody up and down the land was bustling around putting up bunting, baking cakes and planning street parties for her jubilee.

Everyone was keen to buy her a present to say thank you for being such an amazing queen for such a long time, but they did not know what to get for somebody who already had everything!

She already had fifty horses and four dogs.

Count them if you don't believe me!

She already had expensive crowns and gowns.

Which crown do you think she should wear for the Jubilee?

And she already had many palaces.

Which one is your favourite?

Then one day, after much thinking, her son Prince Charlie had the most splendid idea for a jubilee gift.

The very next morning he went on the television to broadcast his idea to the kingdom.

"We should all plant a tree for the Jubilee!"
he exclaimed excitedly into the cameras.

And before you could say,
"Platinum Jubilee,"
everybody far and wide
was planting a tree.

There were green ones, blossom ones and very very pretty ones.

There were fruit ones,
sweet-scented ones and
very very leafy ones.

On the day of her jubilee, Queen Lizzie woke up early because she was too excited to sleep.

As soon as he knew she was awake, Prince Charlie prepared Queen Lizzie the most delicious breakfast. He served it to her on the table next to the palace window.

It was when Queen Lizzie started to drink a cup of tea out of her finest china cup that Prince Charlie opened the curtains to reveal her present.

"Surprise!" he cheered. Queen Lizzie couldn't quite believe her eyes.

As Queen Lizzie peered out of the window, the tree-filled kingdom looked beautiful.

She moved closer to the window to get a better look...

Atop of the branches, were birds singing cheerfully as they built their nests.

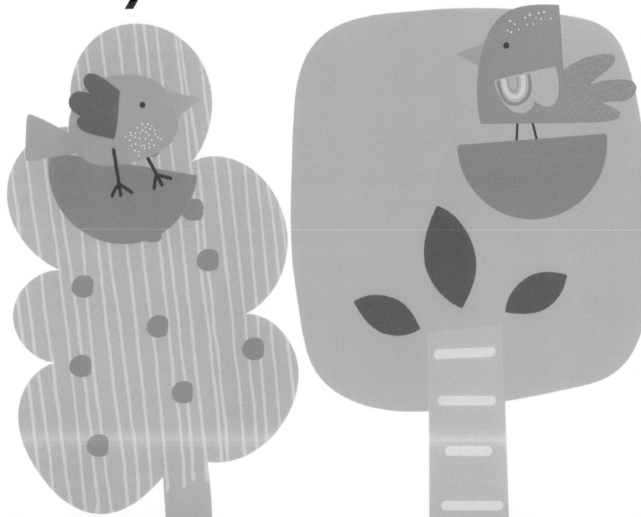

Amongst the trunks, there were children merrily playing hide and seek.

And as Queen Lizzie breathed in with delight, the air felt fresher and cleaner.

"Thank you!" said Queen Lizzie happily. "This is the best jubilee present ever!"

At that moment, the old grandfather clock in the hallway struck 8 o'clock, which reminded Queen Lizzie that she needed to get ready for her day of jubilee celebrations.

And do you know what she wore?

The crown that you picked for her to wear of course!